elusive
equilibrium

<u>an open letter to that m*n</u>

it has been a long, long time
since we have been in contact.

part of me wonders if you
even know you have a daughter

as the last time we spoke i was on bedrest
for a threatened miscarriage.

for years, i feared you.

i kept my whole entire life under wraps
in an attempt to protect us.

it took so many years of therapy to start healing
and working through all my trauma associated with you.

but this letter is me publicly forgiving you.

i never would have been able to create the life
i have now without the birth of my daughter.

she saved me.

and part of me wishes she could have saved you, too.

because i learned, and grew, and rose to the occasion
during my unplanned pregnancy...

while you likely remained the same cowardly,
avoidant person you were.

i still pray for you sometimes.

peace

<u>a namesake</u>
on each and every fragment of a shattered heart
is a name
permanently engraved
like a tattooed signature
or reminder that a part of you will always belong to them
and vice-versa
each name
embodies a memory
not associated with a specific face
but instead a certain emotion
that links every name together
blurring into one unbearable unrequited dream
it takes time
so much time
to rebuild the heart
from the ground up
and no earthly remedy is sufficient
in completely filling the cracks that remain
like ugly scars
but within the spaces of pain and loss
lies room to grow
into something better
eventually being polished
by the rough patches themselves
becoming stronger
wiser, more experienced

until the once-empty void is finally filled
with vibrant, restored hope
and glowing vitality
the names
once bloodily scratched across the tender heart
penetrating like barbed wire
have transformed
into jewels around a crown
or medals hung on a neck
every name
that once haunted you
ruled your life
and stole your sleep
was only a minor character in your plot
every grueling heartbreak
was only a single chapter
and you are the hero
your name graces the cover
in the most exquisite font
and is the most
important of all

lukewarm love
a paradoxical push and pull
of being both too much and not enough
contained in the tiniest box
reduced to nothingness
i am told to stop trying so hard
to just think less
to relax
as if my most genuine qualities
my sacred vulnerabilities
are what need to be dimmed for you to accept me
but
this is the moment i refuse you
shedding all my unfulfilled expectations
that you would return
even half
the energy i gave away

lukewarm is not enough

it was never enough

<u>memory's odor</u>
your name meant fragrance
like the incense you gave me
that i left on your doorstep

the aroma of chai tea
you slicing open the cardamom
with a knife
not quite as sharp
as your tongue

the scent of your room
where solace turned to solitude
and i found myself wanting to be anywhere
but with you

you told me i smelled of coconut
and it made me feel exotic
but i was only a trinket
to add to your collection

i am so much more than a cheap perfume
and you will never know the depth
of my excellence

<u>heart cry</u>
how simple it must be to be a man
to be so oblivious of objectification
as a woman wrestles with her core identity
wondering if she'll ever possess a voice
loud and clear enough to be heard
wondering if she'll ever be small enough
to inhabit a body that isn't sexualized
i am told i am beloved
but i have not yet seen what it means
to be loved unconditionally
i have been loved like a present
too enticing not to unwrap
i have been loved like a punching bag

i have been loved
as though no matter what i wear
what i say
or where i go
i will always be fighting
fighting to keep my emotions in check
fighting to quell my own desire
fighting to face the parallels of past trauma head on
and i am weary
on behalf of women as a whole
of the necessity
of our constant hypervigilance
just to stay alive.
we are meant
for
so
much
more

<u>perfect fix</u>
your fixation: symmetry
the way the tapestry on the wall
had to be precisely circular
to your engineer eyes
makes me wonder
do you scrutinize me
in the same way?
how far my stomach protrudes
or the depth of the stretch marks on my arms?

my fixation: numerical value
weight on scale
daily calories
ounces of water
minutes of activity
all tracked and controlled
on a doctor recommended app
that only illuminates my disorder
we tell ourselves perfection doesn't exist
and yet we strive for nothing less

<u>snowy toes</u>
there was desperation in the air
that night filled with clarity
angry music in my ears
showing up unannounced
you opened up your door
the same way you always did
but the forced casual-ness
was stifling and loaded
i came for one singular item
but instead
you beat me to the punch
and boxed up our whole life together
before you even knew i had arrived

fight or flight
but i was already halfway gone
an image forever engrained
of your bare feet
tiptoeing through the ice and slush
chasing me down
for one last order of business
as if you realized
you would most certainly
never see me again

<u>sacred words</u>
i have been burned in the past
by manipulative
empty utterances
of what i would never
dare to vocalize
myself

"i love you"

but did you really love me?

or did you just hate the idea of losing me

so much

that you stooped so low
to carelessly throw the phrase
into the wind
as one last resort
of hooking me
in your harsh grasp

i once made excuses for you

maybe it was because
you speak many languages

maybe the connotation
of loving someone
is not as universally holy
as i am conditioned
to believe

but now i see

your greatest fluency
resides in your toxicity

and the language you most prefer

is lying

bad feeling
you said
we should cease
communication

so i asked
which part
of my fundamental being
was once again not enough
or too much
to bear

you responded
or lack there of
with a gaping silence
that promoted introspection

i am the first to admit
i am flawed
and wounded
and shadowed
and imbalanced

but i am also
resilient
and courageous
and starlight personified
with a capacity to love
that eternally perseveres

i am growing
and expanding
and healing
with each passing moment

so i apologize
on your behalf
that you will no longer be joining me
on my awe-inspiring journey
of returning
to myself

tw

please stop
it is not considered
a victory
or even lucky
that i avoided
r*pe

i was forced to declare
my "no"
over and over and over
and that is in itself
already a huge loss

loss of safety
loss of trust
loss of bodily autonomy

thank god
i reached a place
where i even had
a voice left to speak

i not only asserted myself
but also had to
reassert and reassert and reassert

i was violated
and shaken to my core
too afraid to even leave

so the fact that you finally stopped
after i became less polite
was not assault
altogether avoided
but assault
even still

so you can say
you are so very sorry
but that does not justify
nor at all lighten
the tremendous burden
of what it means
to exist as a woman

<u>perfect mirror</u>
not quite toxic
certainly tumultuous
but most of all
vividly and vibrantly
alive

magnetic
energetic
kinetic

the pull toward you
never ceases

a glowing ember
neither can extinguish

though both have tried

the galaxies aligned
when we were born

and then we met

our spirits finding
home
rest
destiny

the divine artistry
of our togetherness
fueled pathways
for individual growth
and cosmic expansion

so we could reunite
more prepared
for the sheer power
of our unity

your harmony
my enlightenment

intertwining
into one single
complete
soul

<u>grow up</u>
things have been going well
so my mind creates chaos

or perhaps
a denied truth
comes bursting forth
to shatter the illusion
of us

i know for a fact
you are

temporary

unavailable

a karmic connection
meant to teach me
then be gone

but my heart
aches for you to stay
with everything in me

i know for a fact
if i do not let you go
and create space
i will prolong meeting
the one who will stay

and i will only increase
the agony of separating
you from me

but right now i despise
the one i'm supposed to meet
and i don't want to wake up
from my beloved dream

so i'll put off my pain
one more time
and continue fantasizing
while writing poetry
to ghosts

<u>dream poem</u>

you wanted so badly
to be my savior

that you cut the strings
to all my problems

so you could be the one
holding me together

but i needed to find
my own safety

so i removed your presence

and retied the knots
in my own way

so i could be the one
embracing
my own soul

<u>queen of cups</u>

our paths crossed
and i began believing
in synchronicity

how many signs does it take
to know on every level
one's life path
has been accessed

i have been asked
what do i deserve?
and i had no answer

but then you showed me
potential never seen before

i deserve
matched energy
laughing on the floor
and childlike wonder

i deserve to be safe

i assuredly state my values
mirroring the confidence
your aura exudes

striving ceases
tranquility abounds
and now my heart
can finally
find rest

<u>star crossed</u>

i was almost hit by a car
in the parking lot today

i have been numb for three days
struggling to shed a tear

and part of me didn't care
if i lived or died

my only current comfort
is knowing the depth of my pain

is incremental
compared to your loss

you said i saved you
but no aspect of your life
will ever be
my responsibility

i thank the universe
for sending a shout
after i ignored
the whisper

i am forever my own
source of magic

and you no longer have access
to my excess pixie dust

<u>celestial love</u>

your words caress me
comforting elixir

hold me unwavering
patience like rose quartz

your breath as pure sage
cleansing me of shame

presence like amethyst
you make dreaming bliss

two fiery beings
destined by the stars

our love is celestial

blind fear

fun. flirty. confident.

everything i hardly am
personified in her

for me to appear to be
even a third

of how typical people
are naturally

takes
work. research. mimicking.

i'm tired of striving
behind the mask
i didn't even know i had on

take me or leave me
because i'll never be her
and i can only hope and pray

i'm enough as i am

<u>chasing trust</u>
i gaze at your face
every waking day

storing away
each mark, curl, pattern

my mind's eye
a living diary

i say you are my home
and usually feel it to be true

yet

sometimes i fear i do not know you

how can one
be so familiar
yet so foreign

cultivating safety in a single embrace

but also catalyzing
doubt paralysis

do i believe your every word
as sacred truth

rarely tainted by trauma

or do i follow
the lead of hollow dread
that gnaws away
inside my core

<u>scary story</u>

fear response
versus
wailing intuition

does my inner voice
truly scream this loud

am i internally grieving
the inevitable

or am i simply
self-sabotaging
the only good
i've ever known

how can i place my trust in you

when i am unable to
believe

what my body is begging me to hear

i want these feelings
so badly
to be fiction

that i am almost
unwilling
to open the book

<u>complimentary colors</u>

you are pure sunshine
i am hazy daydream

you turn cloudy
with hidden vulnerabilities

i turn fearful
haunted by past hurt

both require reassurance-

you light me up with optimism
i glow from serving you love

i am your playmate
to share in your joy
and laughter

you are my sounding board
for my loftiest visions
and aspirations

i connect us
with divine intuition

you structure us
with trust and freedom

we both inspire

brimming with
boundless creativity
and insatiable passion

at our best
we are balanced

our auras
harmoniously
synched

<u>death whisper</u>

fool me once
i'll defend your honor
but fool me twice
i'll shatter everything
we once knew

all the most heavenly
words, promises, vows
wither away-null and void
as trust disintegrates
evaporating completely

the first time
i was so forlorn
once the numbness
finally subsided
now i am scorned
the poisonous fury
radiating
where i once detected
a groan of warning

i am most remorseful to my body
who tried her best to protect me
yet i undermined her
convincing myself that you
were my saving angel

and she
a false alarm

there is still a ring indent
on my left hand
but the dent
in my fragile psyche
will fade much slower

you assured
and reassured
every sunrise, every sunset
and into the night
all while contemplating
what would become
our ultimate demise

queen of cups (reversed)

how dare you

come into my life

a saint suit

filled with rats

too many to count

infiltrate my haven

leaving nothing

but bare walls

jagged nails

and my absence

trust is non-negotiable

and so is safety

both of which you stole from me

and you continued to take

long after

the song ended

the curtain closed

and my mind broke

how dare you

after i dared

to love and tend to you

unconditionally

til there was nothing left

but dust

<u>your realm</u>

you came down from above

my knight in dove's wings

watching over my wellbeing

giving up pure peace

to be with me

you say i give you a second chance at life

i say you're the reason i don't cut mine short

trading heaven for hell

to be loved and in love

what could be a greater display of faith

i have been burned and scorned

countless thousands of times

and at first i was suspicious of you

how could anyone prove to be safe

after the rug has been ripped to shreds

out from under my heart

but you

you're the reason i had to know such intense pain

without it, might i take for granted

the earth angel in front of me

thank you

for changing the trajectory of my story

towards hope

♥

Made in the USA
Middletown, DE
14 September 2023

38291094R00026